ABDUL'S STORY

JAMILAH THOMPKINS-BIGELOW

ILLUSTRATED BY TIFFANY ROSE

SALAAM
R E A D S

NEW YORK | LONDON | TORONTO
SYDNEY | NEW DELHI

An imprint of Simon & Schuster Children's Publishing Division

1230 Avenue of the Americas, New York, New York 10020

For information about special discounts for bulk purchases, please contact Simon & Schuster

Special Sales at 1-866-506-1949 or business@simonandschuster.com.

The Simon & Schuster Speakers Bureau can bring authors to your live event.

For more information or to book an event, contact the Simon & Schuster Speakers Bureau

at 1-866-248-3049 or visit our website at www.simonspeakers.com.

The text for this book was set in Absara.

The illustrations for this book were rendered digitally.

Manufactured in China

1221 SCP

First Edition

2 4 6 8 10 9 7 5 3 1

Library of Congress Cataloging-in-Publication Data

Names: Thompkins-Bigelow, Jamilah, author. | Rose, Tiffany, illustrator.

Title: Abdul's story / Jamilah Thompkins-Bigelow ; illustrated by Tiffany Rose.

Description: First edition. | New York : Salaam Reads, [2022] | Audience: Ages 4 to 8. | Audience: Grades

K–1. | Summary: Abdul loves telling stories but thinks his messy handwriting and spelling mistakes will

keep him from becoming an author, until Mr. Muhammad visits and encourages him to persist.

Identifiers: LCCN 2020010309 (print) | LCCN 2020010310 (ebook) |

ISBN 9781534462984 (hardcover) | ISBN 9781534462991 (ebook)

Subjects: CYAC: Creative writing—Fiction. | Authorship—Fiction. |

Penmanship—Fiction. | Muslims—Fiction.

Classification: LCC PZ7.1.T4676 Abd 2021 (print) | LCC PZ7.1.T4676 (ebook) | DDC [E]—dc23

LC record available at https://lccn.loc.gov/2020010309

LC ebook record available at https://lccn.loc.gov/2020010310

For my sons, the heroes in my own story
—J. T. B.

To every child with a story in their heart
and a pencil in their hand
—T. R.

Abdul loved to tell stories.

He told one about the high-stepping kids who collected donations in boots. Another about the teenagers who danced in subway cars. He had one about the bow-tie-wearing man hawking bean pies on Broad Street and even one about the woman who sold water ice from her basement on hot summer days.

Writing these stories was hard, though. Making lowercase *b* face the right way was tricky. *P* and *s*, too.

Silent letters were downright sneaky. How could Abdul know there was an *e* if it never made a sound?

Abdul loved straight lines like the ones his barber shaved.
But Abdul's scribbly, scratchy, scrawly letters never stayed on any line.

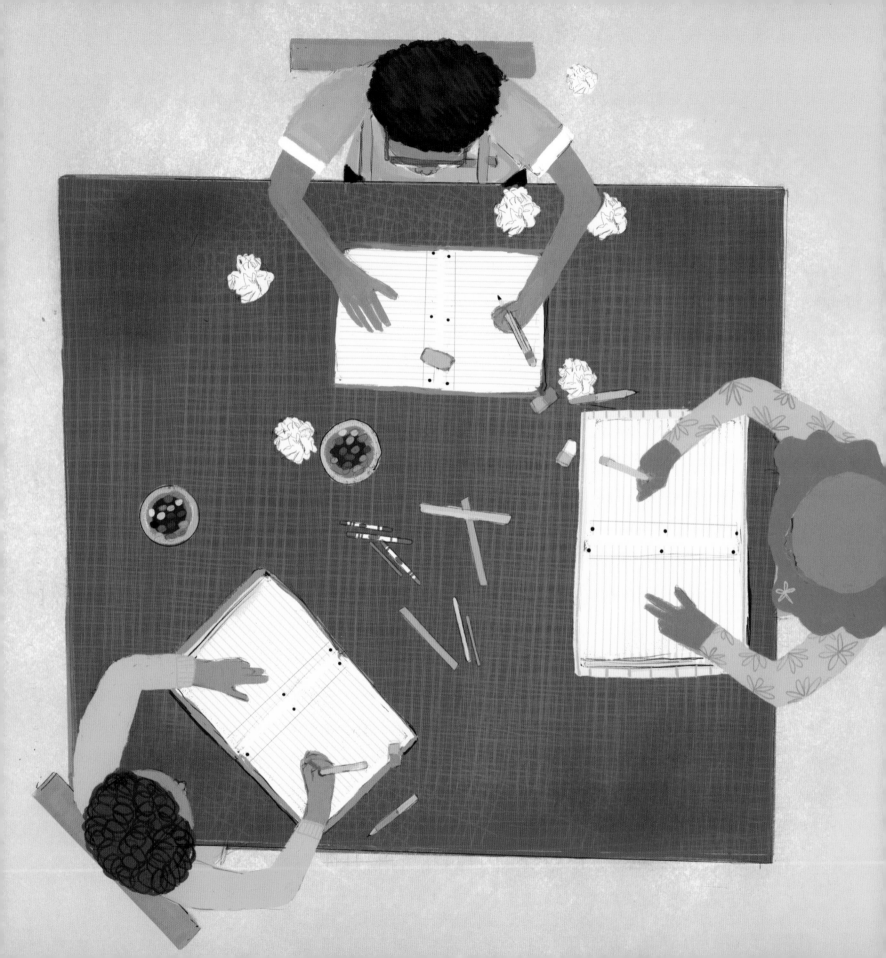

During writing period each day, he wrote, then erased his mistakes . . .
wrote then erased . . . wrote then erased. His classmates
had neat sentences. Abdul had smudges.

Why write his stories anyway? The people and places in his schoolbooks
never looked or sounded like the people or places he knew.

Some stories are for books, Abdul decided, but not his.

One day, Abdul's class had a visitor.

Mr. Muhammad had lines straighter than straight around his beard and hairline. His sneakers, like Abdul's, had not a single crease or scuff. Mr. Muhammad was a writer.

He read a story about a watchful boy with hair shaved low and skin the color of night.

Women braided hair on front steps in this story, girls with clacking beads jumped rope, and men in white thobes prayed on the sidewalk outside a full storefront mosque. The boy watched over this community.

"Write new stories with new superheroes," Mr. Muhammad said.

Abdul pressed his paper down firmly. He could be an author like Mr. Muhammad.

But *b* played tricks again.

Mr. Muhammad walked around, reading each child's work. He was getting close.

Does silent *e* go here? Silent *u*? Erase, erase, erase.

Abdul tried writing neatly.

Write, erase, write, erase, erase, **rip!**

He slammed down his pencil.
Jayda and Kwame had pages
of words. Abdul had a hole.

Abdul slid down . . . down . . . down under the table.
He imagined an eraser big enough to erase himself.

"Nice sneaks! Can I see your story?" Mr. Muhammad asked.

"I don't got a story," Abdul whispered.

"Everyone has stories."

"But I can't write like them." Abdul pointed.

"Me neither," Mr. Muhammad said. "Come with me. I want to show you *my* notebook."

"That's a mess!"

"I get messy words out so good words can come too.
I fix the mess later." Before walking away, he said, "Keep trying."

That gave Abdul an idea. "Bismillah," he said.

SNAP!

Abdul scribbled words and made mistakes without erasing. He wrote around the hole, filling the page.

"I wrote a mess like yours!" Abdul told Mr. Muhammad.

Mr. Muhammad smiled. "Find a great story in there."

Abdul squinted. He saw words, misspelled, but wondrous and sloppy-looking sentences he loved.

Over the next few days, Abdul rewrote a less messy mess, then an even less messy mess. He smiled when he read his story to himself.

But when it was time to hand it in, he didn't feel like smiling.

"That's sloppy!" Jayda said.

"You spelled a word wrong," Kwame added.

Abdul slipped his paper underneath the others.
Some kids are writers, Abdul thought, *but not me.*

Days later, Mr. Muhammad returned.

"I loved your stories!" he exclaimed. "I had to read one again and again. It was so good!"

Everyone sat up. Everyone except Abdul.

Kwame whispered, "I bet it was mine. I spelled every word right."

Jayda whispered back, "He probably liked mine. I have the best handwriting in the class!"

Mr. Muhammad started reading the story in a loud, clear voice. It was about a boy with tall hair, shaped with sharp lines, and skin the orange-brown of sunrise. He watched over the kids stomp-stomp-stepping down the block and the ones breaking to the beat of a city train. He even protected the grown-ups who sold things and were like family.

Abdul sat up. It was *his* story.

And then Mr. Muhammad paused. He frowned at the page. Abdul's cheeks burned. Everyone listened, wide-eyed and silent. Mr. Muhammad read on, stopping a few more times at mistakes, until he reached the end of the story.

"That was by Abdul,"

Mr. Muhammad said.

Abdul slowly looked up. Everyone stared. Were they smiling? Yes! And clapping, too!

"Great story!" Kwame told Abdul.

"I loved it!" said Jayda.

When they returned to their writing, Abdul whispered to Mr. Muhammad,

"What about my mistakes?"

"Writers make mistakes. We'll work on them."

As they worked, Abdul thought:

Some people are writers, and I am one of them.